Jane Hissey

Little Bear Lost

SCRIBBLERS

LANCASHIRE COUNTY LIBRARY

30118132730031

OLD Bear had been very busy all morning. He'd packed an enormous picnic for all the toys. He was just closing the lid of the basket when Little Bear dashed past and dived into a heap of books.

'Do you think anyone will find me?' he called from underneath the heap.

BEFORE Old Bear could answer, Bramwell Brown, Duck and Rabbit ran into the room. Soon they were hiding too.

'We're playing hide and seek,' explained Bramwell from under a cushion. 'Did anyone see us hide?'

'Only me,' said Old Bear. 'Who's looking for you?'

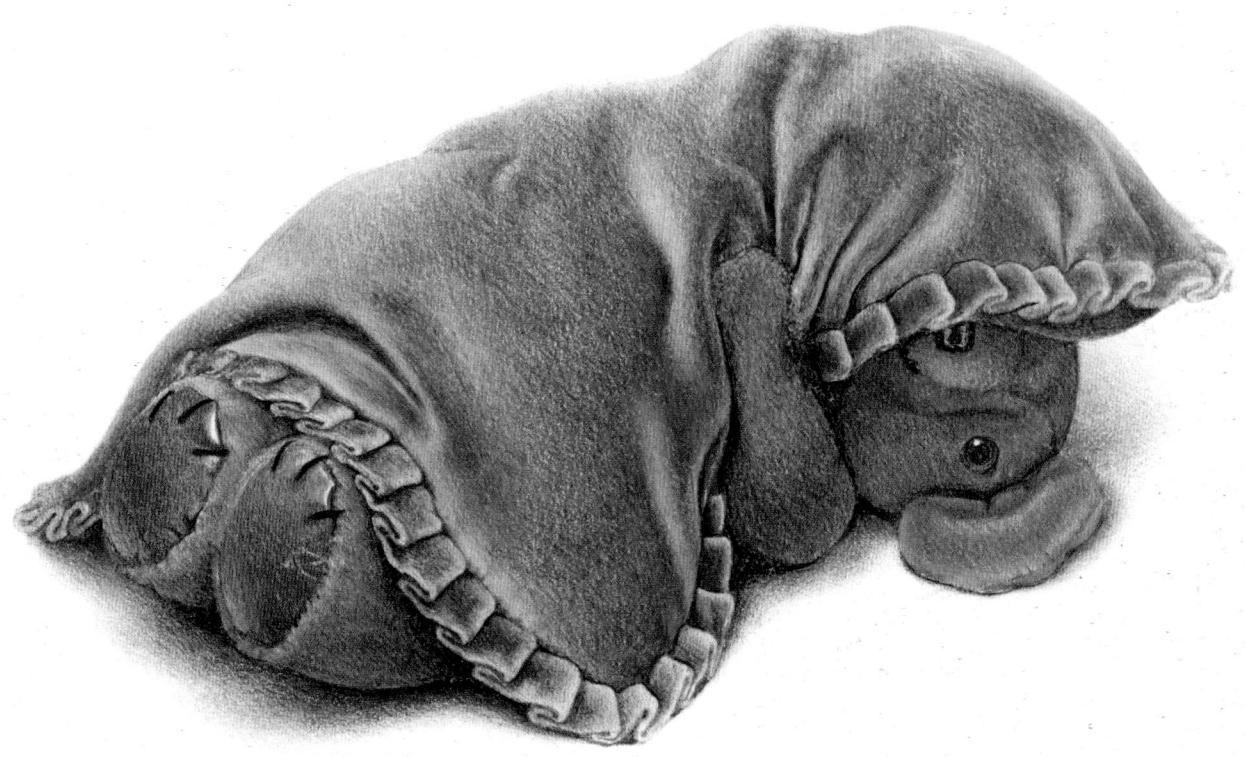

'OH dear,' said Bramwell miserably, 'we've done it again: we've forgotten to get anyone to look for us.'

'That's a pity,' said Duck. 'It could have been a good game.'

'Old Bear,' said Little Bear thoughtfully, 'if we hide again, will you try and find us?'

'Of course,' said Old Bear. 'Are you ready?'

He covered his eyes and started to count.
'One,
 Two,
  Three,' he began as Rabbit jumped into a vase.
'Four,
 Five,
  Six,' he continued, as Duck climbed into a box.
'Seven,
 Eight,
  Nine,' he counted as Bramwell
hid behind the curtain.

'TEN!' he called; 'I'm READY!'
And by then Little Bear had
vanished too.

OLD Bear began to search for the others. First he found a sock that he had lost weeks ago. And then he found ten marbles that had rolled underneath things. He even found Cat, who wasn't really lost or hiding!

But he couldn't find the other toys.

'It's no good,' he sighed. 'I can't see any of you. Can we tidy up a bit and start again?'

THE other toys came out of their secret hiding places, one by one. All of them, that is, except Little Bear.

'Where is he?' asked Bramwell.

'He can't be far away,' said Old Bear, 'Let's call him.'

They climbed on a chair and shouted 'LITTLE BEAR!' so loudly that they nearly fell off!

BRAMWELL peered under the bed. 'He could be here,' he said.

'I'm not going in there,' said Duck. 'It's all dark and dusty.'

'I'll go!' cried Rabbit. 'It's just like a tunnel and I love tunnels.' He was just about to dash under the bed when Bramwell caught him by the tail.

'Take this string,' he said, 'then you can't get lost. We'll all hold the other end!'

WITH the string tied round his middle, Rabbit disappeared under the bed. The others watched and waited.

Suddenly the string gave such a jerk that Duck fell on his beak.

'He's here!' called Rabbit. 'I'm holding onto him. Can you pull us out?'

They all pulled hard on the string and out popped Rabbit clutching, not Little Bear, but . . .

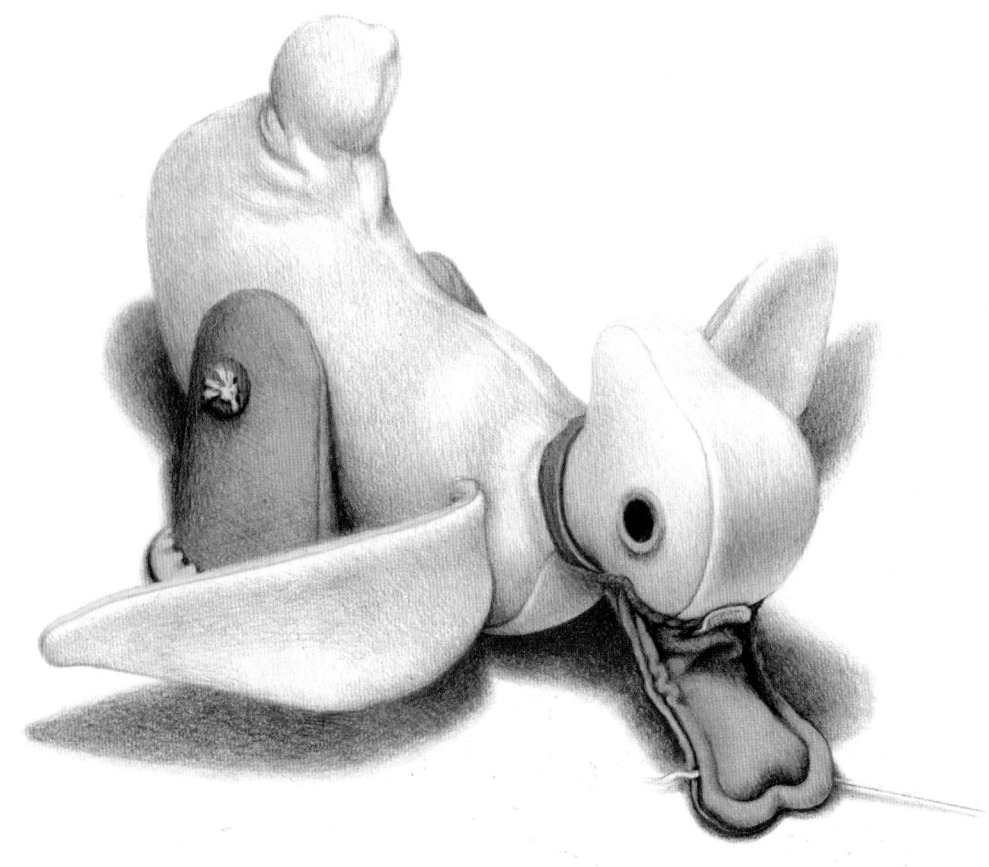

. . . a fluffy slipper!

'Oh,' said Duck, 'I don't think that's Little Bear.'

'It felt like him,' said Rabbit sadly, 'and it was the right size.'

'Never mind, Rabbit,' said Old Bear, 'You did your best. I'm sure Little Bear will turn up soon.'

'LET'S make a poster,' suggested Old Bear, 'with a picture of Little Bear on it. Then everyone will know who we are looking for.'

Bramwell did a painting of Little Bear in his red trousers and made him look a bit sad.

'He does look lost,' said Duck. 'I hope we find him soon.'

BRAMWELL showed his poster to all the toys.
'We need everyone to look for Little Bear,' he said.
They all wanted to help and, within minutes, everyone
was searching. They rolled up rugs and climbed up
curtains. They peered behind plants and jumped into
drawers. But still there
was no sign of
Little Bear.

BRAMWELL sat down on the floor. 'I'm tired,' he sighed.

'And I'm hungry,' said Duck.

'Well,' said Old Bear, 'perhaps we need a little break. We'll have the picnic I packed this morning, then we'll carry on looking.'

He led the way to the basket of food and lifted the lid. 'There,' he said proudly, 'what do you think of that?'

THEY all peered into the basket . . .

'Well, that IS a surprise!' gasped Bramwell.

There, tucked under a teacloth and looking very full, was Little Bear.

Bramwell lifted him out of the basket and gave him a big hug.

'Hmm,' said Duck, staring at the crumbs that covered Little Bear, 'we seem to have found a bear and lost a picnic!'

'Don't worry,' said Old Bear. 'There's plenty left for us! It's picnic time!'

T HEY dragged the basket, bumpety bump, down the stairs and out into the garden.

What a wonderful feast; they finished every crumb!

'Now,' said Old Bear, 'it's time for a rest. It's been a very busy day.'

'No!' cried Little Bear, 'let's have another game of hide and seek!'

But there was no reply. Leaning against the tree and full of food, all the other toys were fast asleep.

For Ivan

SALARIYA

www.salariya.com

This edition published in Great Britain in MMXIII by Scribblers, a division of Book House,
an imprint of The Salariya Book Company Ltd
25 Marlborough Place,
Brighton BN1 1UB

www.scribblersbooks.com
www.janehissey.co.uk

First published in Great Britain in MCMLXXXIX by Hutchinson Children's Books

© The Salariya Book Company Ltd MMXIII
Text and illustrations © Jane Hissey MCMLXXXIX, MMXIII

All rights reserved. No part of this publication may be reproduced, stored in or introduced into a retrieval system or transmitted in any form, or by any means (electronic, mechanical, photocopying, recording or otherwise) without the written permission of the publisher. Any person who does any unauthorised act in relation to this publication may be liable to criminal prosecution and civil claims for damages.

ISBN-13: 978-1-908973-67-2

1 3 5 7 9 8 6 4 2

A CIP catalogue record for this book is available from the British Library.

Printed and bound in China
Printed on paper from sustainable sources

This book is sold subject to the conditions that it shall not, by way of trade or otherwise, be lent, resold, hired out, or otherwise circulated without the publisher's prior consent in any form or binding or cover other than that in which it is published and without similar condition being imposed on the subsequent purchaser.

Jane Hissey

Little Bear Lost

Where is Little Bear?

Where is Little Bear? Bramwell Brown asks all the toys in the playroom, but nobody seems to know. When the toys play a game of hide-and-seek Little Bear finds a hiding place that is so secret, he disappears!

'The illustrations are outstanding, the story safe and reassuring'

THE SPECTATOR

OTHER TITLES IN THE COLLECTION

978-1-908973-18-4   978-1-908973-01-6   978-1-908973-71-9   978-1-908973-17-7

www.janehissey.co.uk

PAPER FROM SUSTAINABLE FORESTS

SCRIBBLERS

SCRIBBLERS
S

ISBN 978-1-908973-67-2

£6.99

9 781908 973672

www.scribblersbooks.com